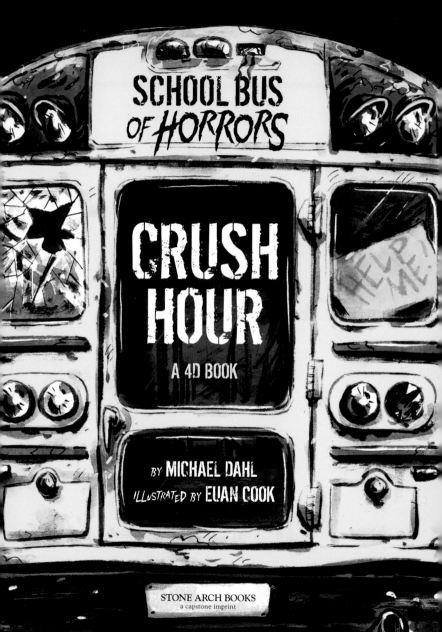

School Bus of Horrors is published by
Stone Arch Books
A Capstone Imprint
1710 Roe Crest Drive
North Mankato, Minnesota 56003
www.mycapstone.com

Cataloging-in-Publication Data is available at the Library of Congress website.
ISBN 978-1-4965-6269-2 (library binding)
ISBN 978-1-4965-6275-3 (paperback)
ISBN 978-1-4965-6281-4 (eBook)

Summary: Row by row, the seats at the back of the bus are squeezing toward the
front. Will Ella and her fellow passengers make it to school before they are crushed?

Designer: Bob Lentz
Production Specialist: Tori Abraham

Cover background by Shutterstock/oldmonk

Printed in the United States of America.
PA021

Download the Capstone app!

- Ask an adult to download the Capstone 4D app.

- Scan the cover and stars inside the book for additional content.

When you scan a spread, you'll find
fun extra stuff to go with this book!
You can also find these things
on the web at www.capstone4D.com
using the password: crush.62692

TABLE OF CONTENTS

CHAPTER ONE
THE VERY BACK........................6

CHAPTER TWO
THE WRINKLED HAND..................16

CHAPTER THREE
CRUSH...................................24

CHAPTER FOUR
THE FINAL SQUEEZE..................30

From dawn to dusk, the **SCHOOL BUS OF HORRORS** rumbles along city streets and down country roads, searching for another passenger. Yellow, black markings, dirty windows—it looks like any other.

But **BEWARE!** Step aboard this bus and experience the scariest ride of your life . . .

CHAPTER ONE
THE VERY BACK

Ella always sits in the very last row of the bus.

All by herself.

Alone.

Ella hates feeling crowded. She hates touching other people.

"People are gross!" she always says to herself.

In the back of the bus, Ella has more room.

No one can touch her.

Ella clutches her book bag to her chest.

Her seat is greasy. The windows are smudged with dirt.

This is not her regular bus.

The other driver must be out sick, she thinks.

Ella hears a deep voice.

"Ella . . . is this yours?"

The strange bus driver waves a notebook at her.

A grimy plastic wall surrounds the driver's seat.

The driver's wrinkled hand sticks out from a small opening in the wall.

"You dropped it on the steps," croaks the driver.

Ella walks slowly toward the front of the bus.

She feels strange as she stares at the notebook.

It is her journal.

CHAPTER TWO
THE WRINKLED HAND

Ella always keeps the journal on the nightstand by her bed.

How did it get here? she wonders.

Ella grabs the notebook from the driver.

She is careful not to touch his
wrinkled hand.

"Those fingers look gross," she
tells herself. "I'll have to wipe off the
book when I get to school."

REEEEEEERRRRRRRKKKK!

A grinding noise fills the bus.

The students turn and look toward the rear of the bus.

The back seat—the seat Ella was sitting on—has moved.

The bus is one row shorter!

The back seat has been pushed forward. It is smashed into the next row of seats.

"*AHHHH!*" kids scream.

They scramble away from the back of the bus.

They crawl over the seats and rush toward the front.

As the students move forward,
Ella steps back.

"Don't touch me!" she says.

No one can hear her over another
grinding sound.

REEEEEERRRRRRRKKKK!

CHAPTER THREE
CRUSH

Ella and the other students stand frozen. They stare at the back of the bus.

The back of the bus slowly moves forward.

The last three rows of seats are crushed into each other.

"Let us out!" scream the students.

The bus keeps moving along the street toward school.

The driver behind the thick plastic wall chuckles.

"We have to get off!" Ella shouts. **"NOW!"**

Each time the bus passes another block, it grows shorter.

More and more kids squeeze into
the front of the bus.

They pound on the dirty windows.
They bang their hands against the
locked door.

REEEEEERRRRRRKKKK!

The bus is squeezed again. Only one row of seats remains.

All the students are crowded together like pickles in a jar.

Dozens of hands and knees and feet crush into Ella's sides.

CHAPTER FOUR
THE FINAL SQUEEZE

Ella's ears fill with the screams
and shouts of the other passengers.

Then the bus stops suddenly.

Ella takes a deep breath to scream
once more.

Maybe the bus driver will finally hear her.

"*LET ME OUT!*"

The doors open with a rush of air.

The bus has reached the school.

Ella and the other students fall out onto the ground. They tumble like pieces of candy from a ripped bag.

Ella lays on the ground, unable to stand up.

"Need help?" asks a voice.

A girl is standing over her.

The girl reaches out and grabs Ella's hand. She helps Ella to her feet.

"I think this is your notebook," says the girl.

She hands Ella the journal. Two words are scribbled on the last page.

"You're welcome," Ella reads the words aloud.

She looks back. The strange bus is a normal size again.

Ella shivers with fear as she watches the bus door creak shut.

But she does not let go as the other girl squeezes her hand.

GLOSSARY

GRIMY (GRIME-ee)—to be covered by a buildup of dirt or soot

GROSS (GROHSS)—ugly or disgusting

JOURNAL (JUR-nuhl)—a diary in which someone writes down thoughts and experiences

REGULAR (REG-yuh-lur)—usual or normal

REMAINS (ri-MAYNZ)—something that is left over

SCRAMBLE (SKRAM-buhl)—to rush or struggle to get somewhere

SMUDGED (SMUHGD)—made a messy mark by rubbing something

SURROUND (suh-ROUND)—to be on every side of something

TUMBLE (TUHM-buhl)—to fall suddenly and helplessly

DISCUSS

1. Why do you believe the author titled this book *Crush Hour*?

2. How do you think Ella's journal got on the bus? What are some other possibilities?

3. Do you think the bus ride was a good or bad experience for Ella? Use examples from the story to support your answer.

WRITE

1. Create a new title for this book. Then write a paragraph on why you chose your new title.

2. Write your own short story about a character getting stuck in a tight space. How does he or she get out?

3. Write about the scariest bus ride you've ever experienced.

AUTHOR

MICHAEL DAHL is the author of the best-selling Library of Doom series, the Dragonblood books, and Michael Dahl's Really Scary Stories. (He wants everyone to know that last title was not his idea.) He was born a few minutes after midnight of April Fool's Day in a thunderstorm, has survived various tornados and hurricanes, as well as an attack from a rampant bunny at night ("It reared up at me!"). He currently lives in a haunted house and once saw a ghost in his high school. He will never ride on a school bus. These stories will explain why.

ILLUSTRATOR

EUAN COOK is an illustrator from London, who enjoys drawing pictures for books and watching foxes and jays out his window. He also likes walking around looking at broken brickwork, sooty statues, and the weird drainpipes and stuff you can find behind old run-down buildings.

SCHOOL BUS OF HORRORS